A Note to Parents and Caregivers:

Read-it! Readers are for children who are just starting on the amazing road to reading. These beautiful books support both the acquisition of reading skills and the love of books.

 The PURPLE LEVEL presents basic topics and objects using high frequency words and simple language patterns.

 The RED LEVEL presents familiar topics using common words and repeating sentence patterns.

 The BLUE LEVEL presents new ideas using a larger vocabulary and varied sentence structure.

 The YELLOW LEVEL presents more challenging ideas, a broad vocabulary, and wide variety in sentence structure.

 The GREEN LEVEL presents more complex ideas, an extended vocabulary range, and expanded language structures.

 The ORANGE LEVEL presents a wide range of ideas and concepts using challenging vocabulary and complex language structures.

When sharing a book with your child, read in short stretches, pausing often to talk about the pictures. Have your child turn the pages and point to the pictures and familiar words. And be sure to reread favorite stories or parts of stories.

There is no right or wrong way to share books with children. Find time to read with your child, and pass on the legacy of literacy.

Adria F. Klein, Ph.D.
Professor Emeritus
California State University
San Bernardino, California

Editor: Jill Kalz
Designer: Joe Anderson
Creative Director: Keith Griffin
Editorial Director: Carol Jones
The illustrations in this book were created digitally.

Picture Window Books
5115 Excelsior Boulevard
Suite 232
Minneapolis, MN 55416
877-845-8392
www.picturewindowbooks.com

Printed in the United States of America.

Library of Congress Cataloging-in-Publication Data
Donahue, Jill L.
Cass the monkey / by Jill L. Donahue ; illustrated by Amy Bailey Muehlenhardt.
p. cm. — (Read-it! readers)
Summary: Cass the monkey enjoys each of the seasons at the zoo where she lives.
ISBN-13: 978-1-4048-2407-2 (hardcover)
ISBN-10: 1-4048-2407-3 (hardcover)
[1. Monkeys—Fiction. 2. Zoos—Fiction. 3. Seasons—Fiction.] I. Muehlenhardt,
Amy Bailey, 1974– ill. II. Title. III. Series.
PZ7.D714728Cas 2006
[E]—dc22   2006003407

Cass
the Monkey

by Jill L. Donahue
illustrated by Amy Bailey Muehlenhardt

Special thanks to our advisers for their expertise:

Adria F. Klein, Ph.D.
Professor Emeritus, California State University
San Bernardino, California

Susan Kesselring, M.A.
Literacy Educator
Rosemount–Apple Valley–Eagan (Minnesota) School District

PiCTURE WiNDOW BOOKS
Minneapolis, Minnesota

Cass is a happy monkey. She lives in a big zoo in the middle of the city.

The zoo gives Cass and the other animals a wonderful place to live. Cass has fun all year long.

In the spring, when the air is cool, Cass likes to jump rope. She counts each jump until she misses.

She also looks for caterpillars, butterflies, and creepy, crawly bugs. She looks inside logs and under rocks.

In the summer, the air is hot. Cass and her friend Tess cool off in the stream. The monkeys love to splash around in the sparkling water.

Cass and Tess also love to climb trees. The sunshine warms the monkeys as they swing from branch to branch.

When fall comes, the leaves turn red, yellow, and orange. Cass scampers up the trees. She picks the prettiest leaves she can find.

After collecting leaves, Cass finds a nice spot in the trees. There she takes a nap. When she wakes up, she snacks on the juicy red apple the zookeeper gives her.

17

In the winter, the air turns cold. It starts to snow.
Cass moves inside. It is warm and cozy there.

Cass likes to watch the snow fall on the city. She wonders what it would feel like to catch a snowflake on her tongue.

21

Cass has fun all year long. But no matter what season it is, her favorite thing of all is to visit with you!

More *Read-it!* Readers

Bright pictures and fun stories help you practice your reading skills. Look for more books at your level.

Alex and Sarah 1-4048-1352-7
Alex and the Team Jersey 1-4048-1024-2
Alex and Toolie 1-4048-1027-7
Another Pet 1-4048-2404-9
Izzie's Idea 1-4048-0644-X
Joe's Day at Rumble's Cave Hotel 1-4048-1339-X
Kyle's Recess 1-4048-2414-6
Naughty Nancy 1-4048-0558-3
Parents Do the Weirdest Things! 1-4048-1031-5
The Princess and the Frog 1-4048-0562-1
The Princess and the Tower 1-4048-1184-2
Rumble Meets Harry Hippo 1-4048-1338-1
Rumble Meets Lucas Lizard 1-4048-1334-9
Rumble Meets Randy Rabbit 1-4048-1337-3
Rumble Meets Shelby Spider 1-4048-1286-5
Rumble Meets Todd Toad 1-4048-1340-3
Rumble Meets Vikki Viper 1-4048-1342-X
Rumble's Famous Granny 1-4048-1336-5
Rumble the Dragon's Cave 1-4048-1353-5
The Three Princesses 1-4048-2422-7
Willie the Whale 1-4048-0557-5

Looking for a specific title or level? A complete list of *Read-it!* Readers is available on our Web site:
www.picturewindowbooks.com